Connect with the World of Mrs. Ashbury in one of the ways below:

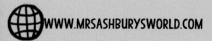WWW.MRSASHBURYSWORLD.COM 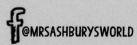@MRSASHBURYSWORLD 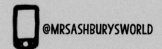@MRSASHBURYSWORLD MRSASHBURYTHEBOOKCHARACTER@GMAIL.COM

Mrs. Ashbury
Teaches Black History

Written by Rekia Beverly

Illustrated by DG

Printed in the United States of America
ISBN-13: 978-1660156641

Dedication:

To my family and friends who helped make this book come to life.

"Boys and girls, it's time to see the wonderful people I have for you to meet," said Mrs. Ashbury.
"Walk to the carpet, and set an example, please. Be a leader and a role model. Making smart choices is simple. It's a breeze."

"Criss cross applesauce! Clap, clap, clap. Hands in your lap, lap, lap."

Mrs. Ashbury smiled and added, "Today is a special day. I've invited all my friends from the past.
Keep your listening ears on because I saved my favorite guest for last."

Mrs. Ashbury continued, "Everyone close your eyes!
It is now time for my first surprise!"

The students opened their eyes, and they were confused. Mrs. Ashbury was sitting in a salon chair and hair care products were being used.

"This is my friend, Madam C J Walker. She created a way to help Mrs. Ashbury's curls stay healthy and in place."

"Hello, boys and girls," replied Madam Walker. "I am glad you invited me here.

I was one of the first self-made, black, female millionaires in the United States.
Who would like to sit in the chair next so I can demonstrate?"

"First, I will use the hair ointment that I made.
A twist here, a twist there, and then a special braid."

Mrs. Ashbury marveled, "An entrepreneur, a philanthropist, just to name a few.
Last, but not least, she was a social activist too."

Bruce shouted, "Wow, Mrs. Ashbury, this is such a great day! Who is our next special guest?"

Mrs. Ashbury responded excitedly, "Okay, okay, okay."

"Oh my! It's getting chilly in here,
and I'm starting to hear cheers."

"Double axel, spiral, toe loop and more," Mrs. Ashbury said.
The class was becoming eager as ice appeared on the floor.

"Sparkles, flare, ice skates, pizzazz.
Welcome to our class, Debi Thomas!"

"Hello, new friends," greeted Debi. "I'm an ice skater, as you can see.
I was the first black person to win a medal during the winter Olympics in 1988, I guarantee!
Not only do I have that accomplishment, but I also became a doctor to help people who may have broken a hip or knee."

Mrs. Ashbury proceeded to the classroom's next special guest.

"This woman attended the same college as me." Mrs. Ashbury smiled and sang, "FAMU, I love thee!
That's Florida Agricultural and Mechanical University to be exact.
You could find her on the tennis courts. Swish, swoosh, clack went the sound of her racket."

"Greetings, boys and girls. My name is Althea Gibson. I was the first black athlete to cross the color line of international tennis."

A hand was raised. Angie had a question. "Was it difficult to pave the way?"
Ms. Gibson reflected and answered, "Yes, it was, but I didn't let them discourage me.
I practiced night and day."

"Ash-bur-y! Ash-bur-y! Ash-bur-y," the class shouted.

Mrs. Ashbury appeared from behind the curtain.

Kaitlyn yelled from the seat, "Is this a concert?"

Mrs. Ashbury replied, "Enjoy the show, we are about to begin."

"ABCD, 123. Knowledge is everything! This time, won't you sing with me? ABCD, 123. Knowledge is everything! Sing it out! Scream it out loud! It's all about the learning!"

The class was rocking to the beat. Mrs. Ashbury paused, "Students, wait one second. I have a friend I want you to meet."

"Mr. James Edward Maceo West, please come out!
I would not have been able to perform my song if it weren't for you.
That's for sure, without a doubt!"

Mrs. Ashbury explained, "Your invention of the electret microphone amplifies my voice.
I can hold the mic in my hand or place it on a stand. It's my choice."

A voice came over the loud speaker.

"Mrs. Ashbury's class prepare for take-off!" The class began to panic.

"No worries, class. Ms. Katherine Johnson has it under control. She's a natural, a pro. It's organic for her."

"Ms. Katherine Johnson? We don't know her," the class retorted, unsure.

"Ms. Johnson is the mathematician to calculate astronauts being able to fly into the air," Mrs. Ashbury ensured.

"She began her career only working with women.

In the past, men and women didn't work together, neither did black and white people," Mrs. Ashbury continued.

"Then, one day Mrs. Johnson's expert knowledge in analytical geometry made the world a believer!

She was persistent and ignored the men being mean.

That's why we should trust her.

She has never failed a mission; she's always been assertive and consistent."

"Boys and girls, I think you will love our next person to enter.
He is an inventor!

Three scoops in a cone, three scoops in a cup. There are so many
flavors to choose from.
Stand up and make a line, class, and please, no touching the glass,"
Mrs. Ashbury cautioned.

One student wanted chocolate ice cream, and another asked for
sherbet. Someone in the back of the line wanted sprinkles on top, and
Mrs. Ashbury was trying to catch a cone that was about to drop!

Mrs. Ashbury began to sing, "Listening ears, listening ears, please listen
to me! I need your attention please, quiet, quiet, please." The class
quieted down as everyone was eating their ice cream.

"Meet Mr. Alfred Cralle, the inventor of the ice cream scoop," Mrs.
Ashbury added. "Hello students," greeted Mr. Cralle.

"Remember this phrase, 1 scoop, 2 scoops, 3 scoops more;
never let your ice cream touch the floor."

The students enjoyed meeting Mr. Cralle
and eating ice cream all in all.

"Blake, Avery, and Xander pay attention please.
1,2,3 come back to me."

Mrs. Ashbury moved to the next guest.

"With only one dollar and fifty cents, our next visitor is someone you will never forget.
She started a school that made a great impact."

"Dr. Mary McLeod Bethune, welcome to our classroom!"

Mrs. Ashbury smiled.
Many students raised their hands. They were intrigued and had lots of questions.

"Where were you born?" asked Jeremiah.
Dr. Bethune shared, "I was born in Mayesville, South Carolina.

I was the 15th child of 17 children, and I was the only child in my family to attend school.
I would go back home every day to teach my family what I had learned because I felt that it was the right thing to do."

Allaina had a question too. "Why did you move to Daytona Beach, Florida?" Dr. Mary McLeod Bethune explained, "I moved to Daytona Beach after I got married.

I wanted to start a school, and I had a lot of faith. I asked for donations and did not give up.

I believed in education, I believed in women, and I believed in civil rights.
I had a vision and worked hard morning, noon, evening, and night."

"Mrs. Ashbury, Mrs. Ashbury," beckoned Londyn.
"Our classroom is now our classroom.
I thought you said you were saving the best for last."

"Oh my, boys and girls. You must look around and see.
My friend, Ruby Bridges, looks just like you and me."

Mrs. Ashbury instructs,
"Ruby, Ruby, stand up, my friend.
Introduce yourself to the class. Don't be shy. We are all kind and say
pleasant hellos and good byes."

Ruby stood up, so proud for the class to see.
She walked to the front of the class with her socks just at her
ankles, not to her knees.

"My name is Ruby. Ruby Bridges is my full name.
At the age of six, I wanted things to change.
I was the first black student to integrate an elementary school in the
South.
I was told be quiet and to shush my mouth.

I had to be brave because some white people did not want me to
attend, I kept being brave and kept going back to school until the end
...of every school day."

"My dear students, it has been a great day full of knowledge! You have met some of my favorite people from the past. I hope in your hearts they will last.

Now it's time for us to determine
Who was your favorite Black History figure?
Let's cast a vote now and establish our winner!"

Select a Black History figure, discuss their accomplishments. How was that person brave?

_____

_____

_____

Vocabulary

word	definition	illustration
Retorted		
Beckoned		
Integrate		
Amplifies		
Entrepreneur		
Philanthropist		
Social activist		

There were 2 people in the ice cream shop. They each scooped 4 scoops of ice cream. How many scoops of ice cream were scooped altogether?

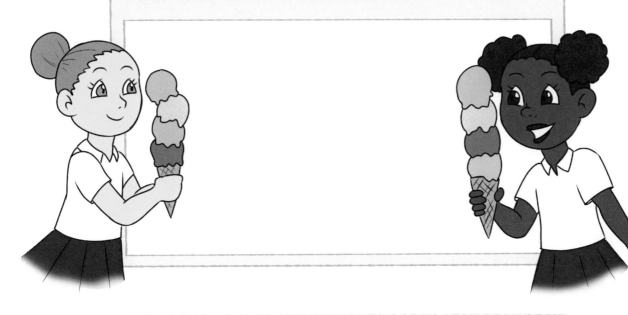

Katherine Johnson helped send 4 space shuttles into space. She then helped 6 more space shuttles into space. How many space shuttles are in space now?

Thank You Gold Sponsors!

Kaitlyn
Bruce Beattie
Angie Meilahn
Londyn Ralph
Allaina and Jeremiah
The Treder Family
The Washington Family

ABOUT THE AUTHOR

Mrs. Ashbury is the brainchild of career educator and writer, Rekia Beverly.
A native of New Smyrna Beach, Florida.
Mrs. Ashbury is dear to Beverly's heart because many of her shared experiences with students are modeled after her actual teaching encounters.
Beverly created Mrs. Ashbury's character as a tool to empower students and parents with a different perspective of how teachers actually view themselves.
Her goal is to give awareness to readers that teachers live normal lives too. They are excited, unsure, and learn lessons throughout the year just like their students.
Beverly is pleased to share Mrs. Ashbury with families and students. Her dream is to continue the adventures of Mrs. Ashbury's class for many years to come.

To connect with Rekia Beverly or inquire about media please reach out to:
mrsashburythebookcharacter@gmail.com

Made in the USA
Middletown, DE
22 May 2022

66077782R00018